CLEO'S ALPHABET BOOK

Caroline Mockford

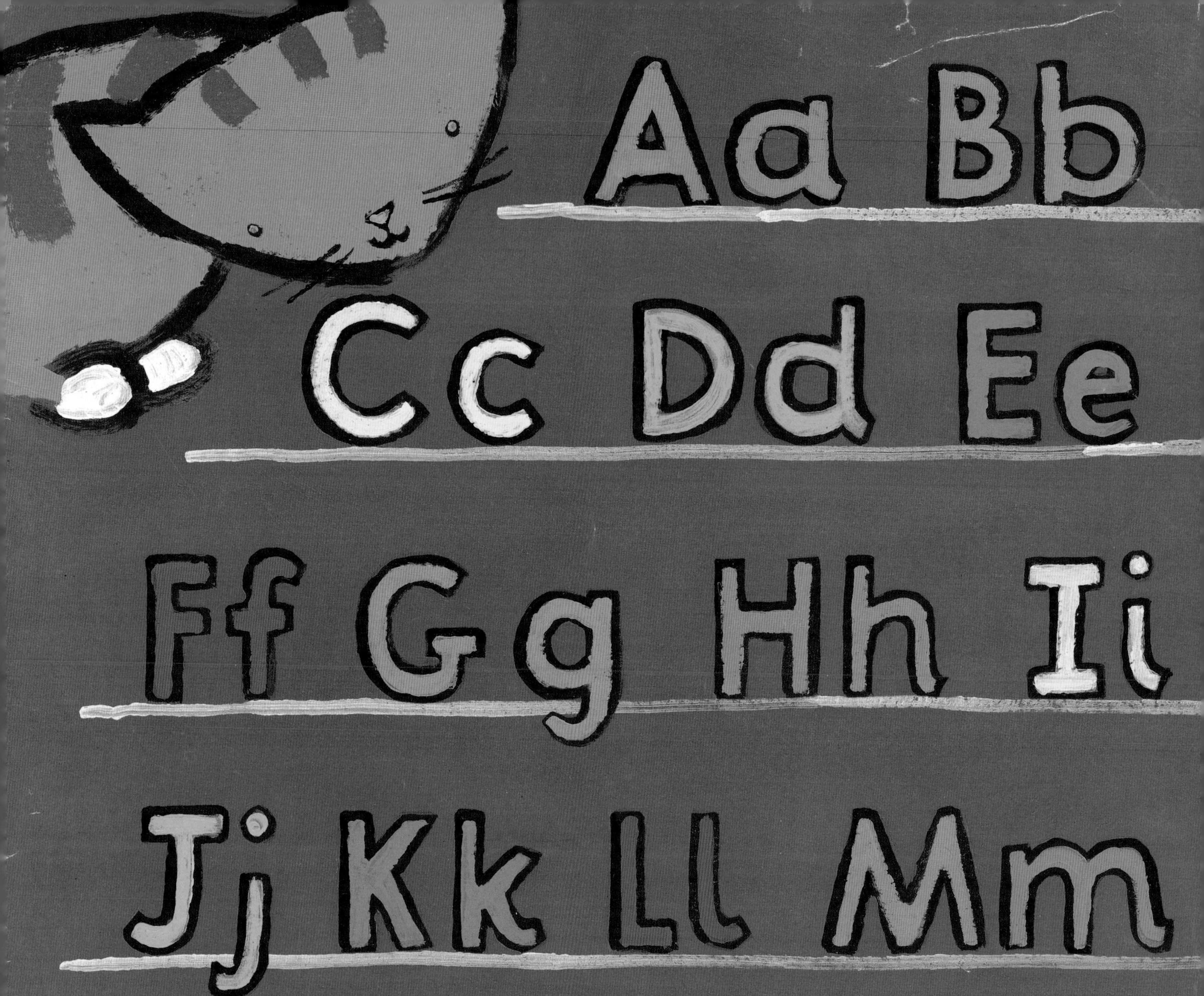

Aa Bb

Cc Dd Ee

Ff Gg Hh Ii

Jj Kk Ll Mm

Let's look at
Cleo's ABC,

Nn Oo Pp

Qq Rr Ss Tt

Uu Vv Ww

Xx Yy Zz

and guess what all
the words will be!

A is crunchy,
crisp and red.

B floats on the waves.

C moos
when she says hello.

D barks as he plays.

E is good for us to eat.

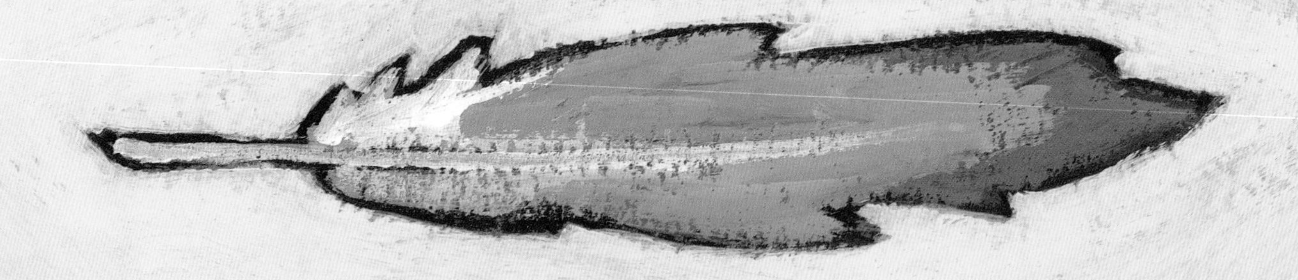

F is what birds wear.

G makes people's
hands feel warm.

Hh
H sits on their hair.

I is round
and made of ice.

J makes toast taste sweet.

K loves
dancing in the wind.

L lights up the street.

M is Cleo's favourite drink.

N is home for birds.

O is juicy, sweet and round.

P makes shapes and words.

Q keeps Cleo
warm and snug.

Rr
R climbs up the wall.

S shines brightly
in the night.

T grows green and tall.

U protects us from the rain.

v drives far away.

W turns round and round.

X is fun to play.

Y means Cleo's sleepy now.
Z means time to rest.

Zzz

Let's practice Cleo's ABC
and all the words
we've guessed!

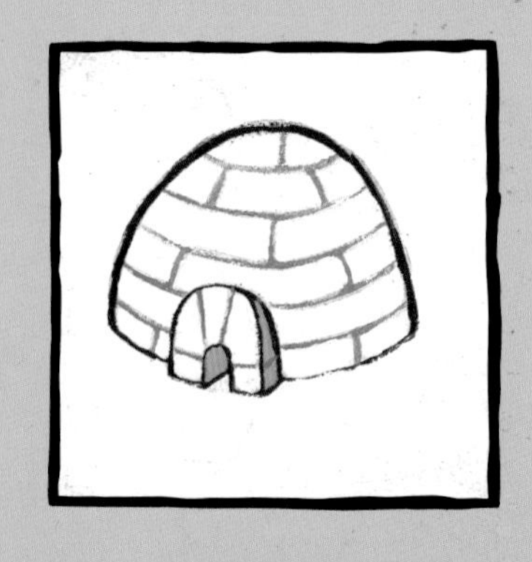

For my mother — S. B.
For Sonny — C. M.

Barefoot Books
124 Walcot Street
Bath BA1 5BG

First published in Great Britain in 2003 by Barefoot Books Ltd
This paperback edition published in 2004

This book is printed on 100% acid-free paper
The illustrations were prepared in acrylics on 140lb watercolour paper
Design by Jennie Hoare, Bradford on Avon
Typeset in 44pt Providence Sans bold
Colour separation by Bright Arts Graphics, Singapore
Printed and bound in China by Printplus Ltd.

Paperback ISBN 1 84148 722 8

British Cataloguing-in-Publication Data:
a catalogue record for this book is available from the British Library

7 9 8